A Very Merry Monster

Lawrence and Keane

Elyse Lortz

Published by Elyse Lortz, 2021.

This is a work of fiction. Similarities to real people, places, or events are entirely coincidental.

A VERY MERRY MONSTER

First edition. December 1, 2021.

ISBN: 979-8201181833

Written by Elyse Lortz.

Table of Contents

Merry merry as they go,

Children rushing to and fro.

What they plot, what weeds they sew,

Oh, how little do we know.

ACKNOWLEDGEMENTS

I would be remiss, and indeed foolish, to not include a heartfelt thanks to those great heroes among us who truly carry the meaning of Christmas in their hearts throughout the entire year. They are a rarity, these bearers of kindness; hidden as veins of gold within walls of cold stone.

Though my inspiration for my books is perhaps not based on these people by name or character, by no means does that then imply I am not inspired by them.

First and foremost, I must thank Brady Penwell, for I believe no one can be quite so truly optimistic of the world than he. I must also thank Cayman Crim, who has known Keane and Lawrence since first the names tumbled from my cluttered brain. Last, but certainly not least, is the Twining family, for, to know the Twinings is to be a great many friends richer.

PROLOGUE

I must first admit this story was nearly lost to the dust and grime of storage. Indeed, had it not been for Mrs. McCarthy's constant insistence that Keane tidy the manuscripts stuffed into her kitchen drawers (the study had grown too full) this tale would not have been put before you at all. My companion might claim it all the better, but I, as a willing accomplice to that Christmas season, would forever mourn the loss. The story itself is, admittedly, of little importance. No great cure was excavated from the murky depths of war. Men continued to send their sons to the front line; creating an epidemic of dead boys to line the soil and allow deep gashes of flesh to plead harbour for voracious prey. Political strategies waged as violent and unceasing as the blood sloshing across foreign lands.

Injuries increased.

Fatalities heightened.

Scars were created and torn open.

Such was the prelude to Christmas.

That holiday season, dampened by war and infamous rationing, remains one of the jewels sparkling in spite of the darkness; a proverbial star that led me forward as thousands of men were thrown back at a hail of bullets. Perhaps that is the very reason I am relieved at this manuscript's brave survival, for it was written in a time in which we were all forced to be brave.

Truly we had embraced the idea of sacrifice for a greater effort. Scrap metal was collected. Old busybodies gossiped around knitting circles, where socks and quilts were manufactured a plenty. Lovesick young women penned hours and hours of verse and sloppy romances to their beaus; steaming with praise for their heroic efforts. Many children turned to Father Christmas to model battleships and pretty nurse dolls, in replacement for the new bike or fashion magazine they would have rather enjoyed. Traditional, brandy-soaked puddings were replaced by carrot cake with a thin layer of cream. Rubber boots were passed down along family lines, just as coats were patched and trouser knees mended. To quote Keane himself, "An old friend is better than a new acquaintance."

That perhaps brings me to one of the greatest gifts I was given that Christmas. It marked the beginning of something far deeper than a mere companionship between myself and the acclaimed professor. A friendship—deep and sure—was sewed between us as songs of great tidings rattled through our bloodied world.

I learned a lesson that year; a lesson which would forever change my life and move me swiftly forward from my child-like naivete to the wisdom and understanding of one well beyond my years. I cannot take full responsibility for this, just as I had no hand in the events as they unfolded.

It merely happened.

It was a simple occurrence neither Keane nor I could expect or control beyond sudden bursts of salvation as we were thrown along.

Yet, it was a time I would treasure to this very day.

And so, with praise beyond myself, and a bow of reverence toward Keane's genius, I lend you the true story of Christmas as it arrived all those years ago.

War.

Sadness.

And, most of all, a monster.

Sincerely,
Jo Lawrence

CHAPTER ONE

-December, 1941-

"I THINK CHARLES DICKENS got it wrong." Keane raised his head from a stack of manuscripts to where I had situated myself in his armchair with a leather-bound novel pressed between my hands.

"Come again?"

"Dickens. You must agree he was a bit of an optimist when it came to a child's innocence. I mean, just listen." I opened the book across my lap and, with a grand flourish, followed my ink-stained finger across the page. "'*For it is good to be children sometimes, and never better than at Christmas, when its mighty Founder was a child himself.*' There, now isn't that at least partially absurd? The poor man is begging for every person on earth to go mad."

"We are halfway there already." My companion grumbled; scraping aside a newspaper bearing the brunt of the world's increasing tragedies. "'*It is well war is so terrible, otherwise we should grow too fond of it.*'"

"Quoting Americans, are we? Must be getting desperate."

"Not at all." Keane quickly amended. "Your General Lee may have had deplorable views, but any man can see the value of life when exterminated on such a disastrous scale." I scoffed.

"Except Hitler apparently." My companion did not respond beyond rising slowly from his desk and stretching the muscles in his hands, strained from many hours clutching a pen. Once satisfied with the usual dexterity of his long fingers, they dipped down into one of the many bowls thrown about the study and brought a cigarette to his lips. In our short acquaintance, the habit of long hours spent in a haze of smoke had overtaken much of his character sketched deeply into my mind. There were, of course, the physical traits as well—greying hair pomaded close to his head with a hint of curls and waves, intelligent blue eyes, and a lithe frame that towered over every aspect of humanity—but these were strictly the basics attached to his formal title.

Professor Brendan Keane: doctor of psychology.

An overbearing cloud had formed from the bitter tobacco by the time my companion decided upon a conversation; this one arising as he prodded half-heartedly through the stack of letters haphazardly abandoned on the arm of the sofa.

"If people spent the same amount on the war effort as they did on holiday cards, all the young men in England and its sisters would be with their families this Christmas."

"Not all of them are store bought prints." I pointed out. "That one seems to be drawn by a child." Keane turned the folded paper over in his hands and studied the crude shapes thickly formed by lines of coloured wax. He smiled as he read the note scrawled inside.

"Miss Jane Whittaker. The girl never travels without her crayons. Ah, and her mother sent a photograph." My companion passed a small sheet of black and white down to me before setting the brightly decorated card on the fireplace mantle. I recalled hearing the name of Jane Whittaker on numerous occasions—I even waited many a time for Keane to return from her house after an appointment—but, as I studied the shades of grey captured between my fingers, I did not recognize the girl at all. She was young, perhaps seven or eight, with long, dark hair and eyes appearing to swallow the rest of her face. Some weeks before, Keane had briefly mentioned the girl's desire to become a revered artist, and indeed the photograph was not much different from the thousands of other children harbouring the same dream.

There was only one abnormality.

Rather than the crayons gripped between tiny fingers, she sat back on the floor with the wax sticks grasped between the toes of her right foot as she dragged it across a piece of paper.

"She and her mother were caught in the Blitz." Keane reached out a thin finger and pointed gently to the empty sleeves of her dress. "Both arms, Lawrence. They were in such bad shape, there was little else to be done. Her father died in battle not a month later." I managed a jagged breath and quickly passed the photograph back to my companion.

"If the entire world saw this picture, armies might throw down their weapons where they stood."

"Perhaps."

"You aren't convinced. I admit it is rather a stretch, but I thought—"

"You thought every human being had the same compassion and remorse as the reformed Ebenezer Scrooge." Keane finished coldly. "I regret to say many remain unchanged and have fallen headfirst into their own graves." This thought had not come to me completely, though, through reflection, I did realise it at least existed. And why shouldn't it?

I might have been marginally concerned by my companion's hand sweeping ever nearer to the fire poker had Mrs. McCarthy not entered with news of the one thing sure to bring about an immediate change in any mood; for better or for worse.

A patient.

Keane stepped away from the fireplace, and I was well on my way toward the hallway when I was shoved aside by a rather stout woman pinched within the height of wartime fashion. She dragged at her side a boy whose face was just as plump and round as his mother's, if not more so, and whose sour expression was only marginally less than that immediately set upon Keane as she stormed further into the study.

"There is something wrong with my boy." I had heard many unusual entry lines in my acquaintance with Keane. My own role as a conversationalist remained something of a social disaster. This mutiny among relatives; however, forced my feet to remain firmly planted just inside the double doors. Keane's posture was a reflection of the same stolidity as he forced the woman and her obese offspring to a halt with a single, raised hand.

"Mrs. Severtson, I ask you to have some decorum. This is a study, not a London department store." I held in a short burst of laughter with the back of my palm.

The vision of Keane milling about with armloads of packages did, after all, hold some amusement.

Mrs. Severtson shifted from foot to foot, much too confused to agree.

"I know that. I was in London just yesterday to meet with Doctor Quinton about poor Reggie here. That man should have his license revoked for the things he said about my son. Shameful. He claimed there was nothing wrong with my boy and that, if I didn't believe him, I should get a second opinion. So here I am for you to take a look at him." The civility of my companion's tongue creaked and groaned as he settled himself at his desk.

"Mrs. Severtson, I have already completed every possible test, and not one indicates any abnormalities."

"But there must be." The obese woman sunk her immense weight upon one of Keane's comfortable chairs; forcing the padded seat downward with a disheartening shriek of leather. "He's an angel of a boy, my Reggie, but sometimes the strangest notions get in his head. A month ago, he broke a school window playing cricket." I chuckled.

"Hardly unusual. Trevor Wilson did the same to Keane the day before last."

"But with a cricket bat?"

"It's possible." I conceded plainly, for, while it would be more difficult than sending a cricket ball through a plane of glass, most anything could cause the same result. Even, on one occasion, Mrs. McCarthy's rolling pin.

My observations were met with an indignant scoff.

"The headmaster claimed Reggie shattered the window on purpose. My boy wouldn't do something so horrid unless there was something wrong with him." Such as a lack of discipline, as the very boy was expressing through tipping a jar of pencils on its rim; forcing it dangerously one way before flinging it back in the opposite direction. Keane winced when the pencils scraped along the glass edge; however, the only loss of control appeared as he folded his hands atop the desk; knuckles blanching slightly as more force was applied to the fingers.

"Mrs. Severtson, I understand it is difficult to come to terms with the idea one's child may be less than saintly; however, what other option is there before us? Is it not at least possible—"

CRASH!

Keane leapt from his seat as shatters of glass scattered across the floor with a rather presumptuous pencil traveling eagerly across the floorboards, pausing mere inches from my booted toe. I gaped at the stick of sharpened wood before jerking my head eagerly at my companion. The natural pallor of his face flushed red across the pronounced cheekbones and bits of the vivid colour had seeped into the veins running ragged across the whites of his eyes. Mrs. Severtson did not so much as manage an embarrassed apology or flinch at the unexpected ruckus. She simply folded a fat hand over her handbag.

"Reggie, you promised you would be careful."

"Wasn't my fault." The boy mumbled; kicking a foot across the shards. "A bunch of fairies made it fall over." A slender hand, white enough to count every vein and muscle, waved me toward the broom closet, where I collected the necessary tools to whisk away the larger pieces of glass. Reggie; however, was content to move on to kicking his feet against the ornate, wooden cupboards running along the bottom of Keane's bookshelves. His mother appeared oddly pleased with her son's behavior.

"See there, Professor? He never settles down, no matter what I say. Wouldn't you call that a medical symptom; being restless all the time."

"That often depends." My companion replied dryly as he nudged the dustbin nearer to where I picked through the more dangerous shards. "In this case, I would venture to say the behaviour is caused by a lack of self-control." Mrs. Severtson leaned forward as far as her considerable bulk would allow.

"You think he's mad then? Should I be getting a prescription or something? A bottle of special 'calming down' pills." God, the woman's knowledge of the medical profession was astounding. Keane strode briskly across the study to pull young Reggie back to his mother just before he managed to climb the bookshelves as a ladder.

"I won't be writing a prescription, as, to my knowledge, there has been nothing invented specifically for annoying children. Lawrence will show you the way out."

And I did.

Gladly.

"That was . . . entertaining." I sighed as the cottage door had closed behind our unwanted visitors. Keane said nothing, having settled once more behind his desk with the strong addition of a glass of Irish whiskey and a cigarette burning in a crystal ashtray. The glass had been properly swept from the floor and Mrs. McCarthy was in the process of carrying the pieces away in a metal tray, only to pause when I entered.

"Sure, if that was my wee lad—"

"He would be a great deal more behaved." Keane finished coolly. The liquor and tobacco had managed to remove much of the anger from his voice, leaving only a tone of general boredom. He was right though. Had the Severtson boy been an offspring of the strong-willed housekeeper, he would certainly know more about manners, or at least he would have a few welts from the brunt edge of a rolling pin.

My shoulder tensed when a wrinkled hand tapped me back to reality.

"Sorry?"

"Sure, Joanna, thought you drifted off for a wee kip, so I did." Mrs. McCarthy smiled. "I was asking about your plans this Christmas. You'll be having dinner with himself, won't you? Or do you have prior engagements?"

"I didn't have any other plans last year."

"Sure, but that's a good many days you could have used making new friends. If you weren't hanging about with that old grump, that is." I smiled and rambled off some noncommittal sentences too inconsequential to remember. It has always been easier to express what might be forgotten, than to state the facts forever to rest in one's mind. In truth, my attempts at acquaintanceships beyond Keane had often started and ended in the same sentence. The few men my age left untouched by His Majesty's Services were more interested in a woman's anatomy than the comprehension of her mind. It was here the use of a RAF jacket and cropped hair held their significance. I had no interest in the modern young things I myself had been confused for on various occasions. The music was enjoyable, but the wild parties and groping dances were certainly not.

I returned to the armchair, as well as the novel I had so ruthlessly abandoned; lulling gradually back into the realm of carefully structured words plodded across each page. Not long after, I folded it once more between my hands.

"If I could write half as well as Dickens, I think I would be very happy." Keane scoffed and crushed the last puffs of his cigarette between those long, elegant fingers.

"Strange to say you would be better off being like a miserable man who, I remind you, has written considerably little of late." I was unsure whether to laugh at the jest, or even acknowledge its existence. In the end, I rallied a tentative smile that lasted the few minutes preceding Mrs. McCarthy's inevitable return. This time; however, she was accompanied by the scent of pine boughs and sweat.

"Mr. Hilling from down the road brought a lovely tree for Christmas, Sir. Will you be wanting it?"

CHAPTER TWO

I did not see Keane again for another three days, and indeed, when I clambered off my motorbike and up the steps to the stone cottage, I did not see him at all.

He was not there.

Mrs. McCarthy, on the other hand, was all too willing to invite me inside, toss an apron over my head, and set me to work chopping nuts and dates, while she continued kneading enormous piles of dough. To say my uses in the kitchen were few is an understatement; however, in menial tasks, I excelled. Recipes were adjusted around wartime rations (though I noticed Keane's housekeeper was able to supply a great deal more sugar and flour than expected), with holiday sweets being pulled from the oven at an alarming rate. At last, I was released to the study.

I must admit the study has always been the one place where rarely a fuss made on Mrs. McCarthy's part. She tidied certainly, but not so diligently as to disrupt the natural disorder of Keane's haven. Books taken from the shelves were left wherever their owner set them in a moment of distraction, not to be remembered for days or weeks on end. Eventually they would be found, though hidden beneath manuscripts, newspapers, or even, on certain occasions, a cup of tea well on its way to the production of penicillin. (The last of these was a rarity I admit only out of the knowledge it did occur on one rather tiresome occasion.)

Keane was, by his own habit, a man careful to maintain dignity in all things. Cleanliness was a necessity, unless the very disorder was itself an order. Items not detrimental were often removed, gifted away, or the first to meet the heavy fist of his temper. Only a few relics of sentimentality remained permanently set; a conservative set of framed photographs (most of which were kept locked in his desk drawers, metals and awards (gathering dust as bookends, rather than due acclaim), and a few handkerchiefs with Keane's name clumsily stitched along the edge (done, I thought by a woman bereft of fine motor skills). Any surviving reminder of his parents was carefully hidden away, if it existed at all. Of course, he must have had parents, though it was all too easy to believe otherwise. He was his own man—a bachelor—and thereby a mystery to all the busybodies tumbling about the town shops.

Keane had stubbornly forgone many of the customary holiday decorations. The colourful greeting cards were indeed set upon the mantle, though no greenery was set around the paper folds. Garland was avoided. Ribbon-wrapped candles appeared only when insisted by Mrs. McCarthy. It was to be expected then that no romanticisms of the season were to be followed as well.

But Keane did have a tree.

It was bare — as naked as a pine ought ever to be — but it was there; standing magnificently in the furthest corner of the room, where Mr. Hilling had wrestled it into place a few days prior. Mrs. McCarthy had ridded the hall carpeting of the green needles; however, I felt the tree was left rather to its own devices soon after. A puddle of fallen greens pooled around the rigid trunk, just as the placement of a window just behind made the branches seem even more bare and lifeless; a tree entirely bereft of joy.

It was dead.

Lifeless.

Expired by the woodman's axe and sent to its maker.

A few other depressing phrases tumbled through my head, but I thought them best left without thought beyond a simple, unchangeable fact.

We all must die sometime.

But everyone deserves a good funeral.

Perhaps, with a bit of paper and paste, I could create a chain or two, wrap it around the more exposed spots, and—

"Ah, Lawrence." I spun around immediately, in spite of the constant insistence I was always welcome at the cottage and rather as much an inhabitant as the owner himself. My boots had, no doubt, twisted the ornate rug in such a way the edges curled over the wooden floor, but it was not my own footwear, or even person, that forced a muttered gasp up from my throat.

"Good lord, Keane. Did you fall in a swamp?" The fact there were, to my knowledge, very few marshes in the area, directly eliminated my excuse for my companion's appearance.

Though a stubborn part of me could not ignore the possibility.

His once polished, brown shoes bore heavy clumps of mud, damp and frozen at the edges. From the cuffs of his trouser legs to his knees, dark water and grease dripped down into his sodden socks. The remainder of the damage was quickly categorized as well. Hat gone. Hair sticking out in all directions. Jacket rumpled and reeking of motor oil. Waistcoat unbuttoned. Necktie loosened. Face smudged with an equal amount of black and brown and a strange assortment of greens. In fact, I found I could only hope the long streaks of brown along his overcoat was only mud.

Keane fumbled with his overcoat, allowing it to fall gracelessly to the ground before lifting it once more at arm's distance and glaring at every possible stain against its majestic countenance.

"Young Reggie Severtson and his troop thought running a line of nails along the road would be the equivalent entertainment of a double feature." He grumbled. "I fear my motorcar did not find the act as humorous."

"Nor its driver." I added drily. "Did you walk the rest of the way back?"

"Only three miles. John Macdonald kindly gave me a lift the rest of the way in his swine cart. I fear the effects have ingrained themselves into my trousers. A pity. I rather liked this suit." I might have added some sickeningly optimistic statement, had Keane not excused himself, only to return moments later with a fresh suit and its injured brethren carried out in a metal rubbish bin. The sight could not be more heart-breaking were the painted can a pine casket carried atop the thin man's shoulder.

"It could have been washed." I tried as he returned without the fabric corpse. "Mrs. McCarthy is magic at mending catastrophes."

"So says the young woman who drives a mound of metal straight from the scrapyard."

"It's a motorbike, Keane, and rather a good one at that. Would you care to borrow it while your own automobile is being fixed?" Oh, what joyous pride unfolding at the slight pallor shooting along his face.

"Plotting to kill me off so soon?"

"Not at all. It was merely an offer made out of the kindness of my heart."

"Kindness, eh? Fortunately, I had the foresight to accept a similar offer from Major Burke. His chauffer surely will have the common sense not to arrive on one of those confounded masses of twisted metal." I brushed the harmless jab at my motorbike far from my mind as Keane settled himself behind his desk with a fresh pile of essays. Every once in a great while, though still more often than he would like, Keane was requested to oversee a course at various local universities. Frequently the semester would create important lessons or subjects we would toss about in curiosity. Opinions were always safe in that study, so long as they were upheld by legitimate facts. It was a system I had learned to apply with deadly precision.

His students; however, ignored his warnings.

"Fairy stories!" He exclaimed suddenly, tearing me away from a particularly thrilling tale penned across a scrap of cheese paper. "These papers are nothing but watered brains soon to infect the vast system of the working society."

"'*All minds must start from somewhere.*'"

"Who said that?"

"You did. Last week."

"Ah." Keane leaned back in his chair and followed my gaze past the corner of my eye and onto the pine towering well over my head. A pen marked the distance in the air. "I haven't the time to decorate it. In all my years in this cottage, I can recall only one other occasion in which Mrs. McCarthy blatantly insisted on a tree. Why she would do so now is beyond me." I recall shrugging absently, while still allowing the shadow of another evergreen to come to light in my mind.

"You had a tree last year. It wasn't quite as nice as this one, but there *was* a tree. I remember it."

"That," Keane agreed with a sigh. "Was the one other occasion." How strange it is to recall that Christmas past. Stranger still to have it marked upon one's mind as an event officially marking the movement from a mere acquaintanceship to companions. Friends, even. I would have thought that an occurrence hidden within the decades; solidly cemented in the eternal threads of time.

Yet, I had not come into existence, while the cottage indeed had.

That must have meant Keane had over ten years of Christmasses without a tree. Without ornaments or celebration. Without the jovial parties we both did our best to avoid. I knew, at least, he did have friends. Perhaps they were not the chummy kind you saw in pubs—thousands of stories poured over a few pints—but their names often rang through the cottage; giving them light and life where else there might be none but the gentle brushes of philosophers long since dead and buried.

Had Keane even celebrated Christmas?

I ran the end of one of the empty branches over my palm; pricking the sheet of skin with the long, green needles.

"Will Mrs. McCarthy decorate it, you think?"

"Probably." The voice behind me begrudgingly conceded. "She did so last year. I would hardly think her to change now." He was right, as usual. Come Christmas day, I had no doubt Keane's long-suffering housekeeper would have, not only the tree brought to the highest of holiday festivities, but the rest of the house as well.

My companion's arguments to such a task would exist, but without any sting or thorn.

There were such things in life one comes to expect; to understand and accept without rebuttal. The world had come to accept war. Children would hardly know any difference as the blood-shed carried on for another year, at least, though probably a great deal longer.

I would know no different.

I stormed out of the study and rampaged down the hall in search of crates and boxes clearly marked with heavy, black print.

"Lawrence—"

"If you won't get in the holiday spirit, I bloody well will!" In truth, I had no idea where to search for Mrs. McCarthy's hoard of little red and green baubles hung about strings of pine the year before, though I quickly deduced they were not in the coat closet.

Upstairs perhaps?

I romped up the ornate, wooden staircase; leaving my companion to tidy the puddle of outerwear left strewn about the floor. Worn coats were tossed freely into the darkness before the footsteps followed me, long strides swallowing stairs two or three at a time, onto the landing. At some point, as we passed along a short row of closed doors and hidden secrets, Keane passed me and continued onward toward the wall's end. An arm came up, a thin ring clasped between his long fingers, until, very slowly, a panel of the ceiling simply broke away from the flawlessness; bending downward into a hatch.

I must admit, I gaped a bit.

As unusual a man as Professor Brendan Keane indeed was, his surprises were never less than . . . surprising. A step ladder appeared, quickly accompanied by the very boxes for which I searched. There were three in total. The first two contained slightly muddled ornaments formed from paper honeycomb. A relec, perhaps, from two decades gone past; back when the first war had ended and the joy of its passing was yet to disappear. I very much doubted these to be Keane's own possessions, but rather the leftovers of Mrs.

McCarthy's overflowing collection. However, I did not think it to be a deception of the eye that so allowed so gentle a brush of his elegant fingers along the contents of the third box; glass figures and shapes skilfully painted with an artist's patient hand. A thin forefinger carefully traced a line of red, deterred to a streak of green, and finally flew away completely with a gentle pat to the side of the box.

"Best get to it, Lawrence." Keane briskly closed the upper hatch with the tips of his fingers.

Away flew all imaginations of my companion's past. Away with the winter winds and scents set to greet the new season. Everything disappeared, including the footsteps quick to retreat down the staircase; leaving me abandoned with the three boxes and the ominous stench of housework.

"JOANNA, SURE I THOUGHT you were opposed to this sort of work. The tree looks beautiful, so." I grinned unashamedly as I stepped back from the once bare pine to revel in the majestic branches heavily decorated with both paper and glass. I had forgone any strings of lights, as only one strand worked, and instead tugged a lamp nearer to the tree. The silver glowed from the yellow light; bright and shimmering against the more reserved colours of the room. Truly there was some pride to be displayed over the work; however, the gauntlet fell more toward Mrs. McCarthy than myself. "Sure, wouldn't you say she did a fine job, Sir?" Keane, who had remained at his desk for the past several hours, forced his eyes to separate from his pen.

"Very nice."

"Sure, Sir," Mrs. McCarthy gasped. "Couldn't you be doing better than that? Joanna put more than a wee spot of work into that tree. You should be saying a mite more than 'very nice'. Why, in Paris, you might give her a wee kiss on the cheek—"

"Mrs. McCarthy!" The housekeeper's face stretched into a smile, while my own turned a deep shade of red. Were she a man, I might have slapped her, punched her; anything to bered the world of such a thought.

Any action beyond a firm handshake simply felt . . .

Unnecessary.

Fortunately, the desperate calls of baking gingerbread tore Mrs. McCarthy away before she could physically force Keane and I into close proximity. The frustrations ministrated prior in the day once more were reflected across my companion's sharp face. The forehead blanched considerably where brief strands of greying hair broke free from its pomade. His eyes had become stone as well. Everything about himself grew absolutely still.

Except for his hands.

I closely observed the pale ends of his fingertips as they searched and dove for the silver cigarette case; working the metal clasp open before pressing a single roll of fine tobacco between his lips. How often I was fascinated with his precise movements. A match or lighter was brought forth with great strokes; clean and sure beneath the end of a cold cigarette. The light hiss of that first draw was always a second's breath from the soft cloud of tobacco yet to come. One might claim the clouds of the sky—gentle and full—to be the thing of miracles; however, it was to my thorough belief this title might fall to none but the thin trail of Keane's cigarettes. Even as anger tugged ceaselessly at his sleeves, the inhales were seldom more violent than the exhales. All things were evenly and rightfully balanced. All things were secure.

All things were safe.

I counted to the third cigarette before the breaths calmed slightly; cogs and gears slowing gradually to meet the relaxing of the lungs. It was then, and only then, my companion spoke once more.

"I had no intention of offending your work. The tree does look quite splendid, should a tree accept such a compliment. Perhaps you will be credited on its behalf?"

"Don't risk a heart attack on my account, Keane." I responded with a daring smile. "As Mrs. McCarthy is absent, I may confess I hated every minute of it."

Victory.

A grey eyebrow rose quickly upon his forehead.

"Indeed? Then why, might I ask, were you so insistent?"

"Because I had never decorated a tree before. Not a proper one."

"Not even as a child?" I shook my head quickly.

"Certainly not. Christmas . . . Christmas is perhaps not a holiday I understand."

"Yet you persist." Keane prodded further. "You decorated the entire monster of nature without so much as a word of complaint." My eyes searched his blue irises from across the room; stepping forward ever so slightly to make certain my expression was shown strong and sure, without any of the nervousness I often faced when attempting to be philosophical in the presence of a true philosopher.

"Keane, it is safe to say neither of us are strictly English—you are an Irishman, while I am a born American—however, this is one of those times I feel the British upper lip is indeed best." In hindsight, it is never wise to tell a man who fought for Irish soil that England's staunch beliefs may hold some grain of truth. Keane, to my good fortune, has always been a reasonable man. Any instinct of offence was washed away by a deep, rough chuckle settling deep in his chest. The cigarette between his fingers was crushed into a filling ashtray before my companion moved off toward a glass decanter to pour two even glasses of brandy. The first of these was gently pushed toward me. Keane gradually migrated toward his leather armchair.

"Lawrence, I find I require your advice. I am at odds to know what to do about that Severtson boy." I sipped at the amber liquor cradled between my hands.

"The local constabulary—"

"Can do very little. He is a child, Lawrence. A worrisome one, I admit, but a child all the same." My companion downed the contents of his own glass before pouring himself another. Rather than immediately finishing this as well, he set it off to one side and folded his thin, tapered fingers together over his right knee. "Reggie Severtson is most certainly not deranged, beyond the trials of early adolescence; however . . . "

"You think there may be a chance he is mad." Keane scoffed; head tilted back against the seat and eyes closing ever so slightly, as though pained by the room's lighting.

"There is always a chance. No man is ever truly sane. It is all a matter of what we do with our insanity that makes all the difference."

"And lining a street with nails is not a good choice, I take it?" My companion's gaze traced a line from the filthy, brown shoes wrapped in week-old newspapers to the worn house slippers that had eagerly taken the place of their predecessors. For the briefest of moments, I expected some great revelation; a few lines to set the world on its proper axis. To tell the entirety of the human race that Professor Brendan Keane had indeed existed, with his mark engraved into the lives of all.

I was sorely disappointed.

Keane rose, kicking away the slippers and striding rapidly toward a pair of old boots left dejected in the hall.

"Get your coat, Lawrence. We are going for a walk."

"A walk?" I spluttered. "But you just walked several miles—"

"And I can manage several more. Here is your jacket. Gloves. Do you have a scarf?" Indeed, I did not; therefore, it was one of Keane's own lengths of knitted wool that was tucked about my neck as he dragged me out into the cold. Sharp shocks of winter air attacked my senses. My eyes watered. My ears stung. My nose too grew decidedly pink, though the pain remained somewhat abated by the familiar scents of tobacco still left in the scarf.

Keane appeared in a similar state and, though perhaps less affected by the cold itself, clearly allowed the exhaustion to make up for it. His long stride remained strong, but slightly slower. The irises of his eyes remained sharp, but slightly bloodshot at the whites. There was everything there, between my own discomfort and my companion's, to insist that we turn round and return to the gentle warmth of the cottage.

Of course, I dared nothing of the sort.

Along we trudged, our miserable pair, toward rock cliffs and the monstrous waters below. The greens of plants were long since dead; not to return until spring once more. A large boulder, placed by God a safe distance from the cliff, looked down upon the raging world. Many a time had I looked toward the sky from that spot. My head allowed to lull back against the stone, I found peace in connected clouds and stars with the pad of my forefinger.

One I thought to see Keane do the same.

I slammed into my companion's back.

My feet were nearly lost beneath me as I staggered backwards.

"If you wanted to toss me over the edge, you might have just—what on earth are you doing?" He had climbed to the flattened top of the large stone, pulling his coat tightly around his shoulders before offering me his hand. With only a slight delay, due to my more conservative stature, I was soon beside him; half-frozen and well on the way of becoming irreversibly so. The leather of my jacket fought valiantly against the cold, but His Majesty's Royal Airforce can only do so much. Keane reached again for his cigarettes.

"Before I begin, I must know how familiar you are with the Severtson family."

"I only met them a few days ago."

"And what was your impression?" I shrugged slightly; burrowing down into my coat the moment my neck met the cold hand of winter.

"The mother seems barmy enough, which would also explain the son's erratic behaviour."

"'*Erratic*', my dear Lawrence, is hardly the word for it."

"Hyperactive, then." I corrected. Suddenly, a strange thought struck me with a violent blow. "His father isn't Sebastion Severtson, is he?" Keane's spine sharpened slightly.

"You know the man?"

"I know of him." For indeed, who did not. There was not one, save the crying infants swaddled in their cradle, who was not familiar with the name. Ministers insisted there was a time in which the man was indeed a being recognizable as human. "The man's a monster."

"Lawrence—"

"An ass, Keane. Sebastion Severtson is a pompous ass who rules the local businesses with less of an iron fist than a bucket of dirt. He has forced no less than three men to comit suicide."

"It was never proven." My companion sighed, though, by the emptiness of his voice, I found there was no conviction threaded within his words. If the truth of men was not enough to sway him, my own carefully recollected events were the epitome of belief. When Keane spoke again, no person could deny the good of it. "I was once asked to be a witness for a wedding. Not some profound, expensive affair, mind you, but a quick fumble of registry papers and rings bought within the very hour. I was returning from a meeting when the man pulled me in; dragging me to one of the pews with the promise it would only take a few minutes. They were both young, but him seemingly more so. He was the sort of man who never gains maturity, no matter the years marked behind him."

"Sebastion Severtson."

"Precisely." My companion leaned forward slightly to catch the flame against his cigarette before continuing. "I have seen him on precisely two occasions since. The first, as it happens, was a Christmas party thrown by a few of the more elite businessmen of London. I had been invited merely on a friend's good intentions, while Severtson had arrived purely out of ambition. He was so caught up in his own work, it would be of no surprise should he not be aware of his son's existence. The second meeting was not nearly so ostentatious. I cannot tell you the specifics—professional discretion, you understand—but I can assure you it was a matter that would forever make the Severtson name unwelcome to the house of Kent, as well as my own."

"Kent? Johnathan Kent? Wasn't he the man who was sent away to—"

"A mental institution, yes." The hollows of my ears filled in one thorough rush before quieting once more as a nauseousness held deep within my stomach.

A month or so, the name of Kent became known to all of Devon as a shameful chain laid upon all kin when Johnathan Kent managed to hang himself on the stroke of midnight heralding his thirty-fifth birthday. According to the article, he was survived by both wife and son, though they had died in the eyes of elite society long before.

I cleared my throat and loosened the lethal grip my fingers had maintained against the tail end of the woollen scarf pulled a bit too snugly about my neck.

"Mrs. McCarthy once said Kent attempted to shoot Severtson as part of a mental breakdown."

Keane's hands went still. His eyes locked forward at the teetering edge of life without seeming to take so much as a breath as departure from the nerve's inexplicable sedative. I observed this, scarcely daring to move lest I interrupt a scene to which I was not yet a part.

At last, his hand crushed away his cigarette on the stone and allowed it to fall lifeless to the hard, frozen ground.

"Yes, she would think that."

"But it isn't true?"

"No."

"But, Keane, even the newspaper article stated—" In a flash of heavy wool and burning nerves, two hands grasped my shoulders. There was no pain in the action. On the contrary, for a man rarely demonstrative in most every nature of the word, he was extraordinarily gentle.

To be gentle; however, never means an action to be less compelling.

In my shock, I found he had lowered his face that it no longer towered over me, but instead bore great holes into my eyes. I was torn between the painful desire to look away, while at the same time distracted by the clarity of the pale, blue irises.

The determination in his voice did little to ease the tension in my shoulders where they remained just beneath his fingertips.

"There are things a man feels he must do in his life. They may not be right in the end, they may even be made so stubbornly they were doomed to fail from the start, but he must do them all the same. This is not a moment of madness. It is merely life—horrible, *real* life—that takes what it can and gives with a closed fist." The long hands slipped from my shoulders to my arms, then were jerked away completely as Keane regarded me critically. Gradually, he nodded once. Twice. "You shall do very well in life, Joanna Lawrence. Very well indeed."

And, with the hope of God and man shining upon my brow, Keane climbed down from the rock, adjusted the lapels of his coat, and trudged slowly back toward the cottage.

CHAPTER THREE

"*'Surrender now, or I shall cut off your head.'*" I made a wild slicing motion with the flat of my hand; pausing at my victim's neck before lowering it to my pockets and tossing the loose, typewritten pages onto the desk behind him. "Well, Keane, what do you think?"

My companion deftly raised a hand to the knot of his necktie as he reached for the abandoned manuscript.

"It is hardly original."

"But—" A raised palm appeared.

"That is not to say the story is poorly written, only that no publisher would accept the piece. A ship captain and a pirate? Really, Lawrence. I would have thought your imagination above all that nonsense." The muscles in my neck tensed. I reached for the paper, only to find it somehow beyond my grasp.

"Captain Moore is no ordinary ship captain."

"Indeed not. Your pirate; however, is quite stereotypical."

"And I suppose you are an expert on pillaging monsters?"

"Yes, rather. You need hardly be lost at sea to discover the leeches wandering about society."

"Like Sebastion Severtson."

It had been nearly a week since last the man's name appeared; however, what had remained unspoken did not stay far from my mind. No longer did I find a dislike for the man. Instead boiled forth a genuine disgust I cannot attribute to any fault but that of a complete lack of human decency.

There is a look in one's eyes, I think, when so great a mood befalls a person. Or perhaps there is merely a breath steadied too quickly against one's own lips.

Whatever it was, Keane saw it.

"Lawrence, you must not hate a man for what you do not know." I raised my head in abrupt defiance.

"I didn't say I hated him." The man towering over me sighed deeply as he slipped his hands neatly into his pockets.

"People rarely admit to hating another human being unless they do not mean it. Take me, for instance."

"You?"

"If I were to tell you I have watched men die by my own hand, would you hate me?"

"Of course not. You were a in a war."

"War is no excuse for mindless killing, Lawrence. I fought because I was told it was for the best; that shooting bullets into other young men was acceptable because they were born in a place different than myself, or that the politicians' game of chess was somehow righteous in eyes better than men."

"Isn't it?" My mind stuttered briefly. "Aren't we supposed to defeat the Nazis? Damn it, Keane, they are burning human beings!" The scent of Keane's tobacco smoke still lingering slightly on his jacket suddenly became all the more bitter. Normally light, vanilla undertones darkened to the sickening odour of flesh crumbling to ash amidst the screams of children and bullets.

My companion's hand shot out, but I managed to step from his offered stability. I did not fear him, for indeed I did not believe such a thing to be possible; however, in the turmoil of my mind, I remained unsure of which line to repeat. Or should I repeat any at all? No words but my own seemed appropriate toward this moment.

Yet my words would not come.

Keane watched silently as I paced; measuring out each stride as I went. To the fireplace. Five steps. The corner. Seven steps. The stack of books. A step and a half.

I stopped when the first traces of light cigarette smoke touched the air.

"You have no compassion then toward the Nazis."

I stared—no I *gaped* at him.

"Should I?"

Before an answer was able to solidify or destroy all that had been carefully created, a shriek erupted through the walls.

Keane had lifted the receiver of the telephone within eight, long strides.

I could have left, then.

At the moment, I considered it to my benefit to do so. I reached for the jacket I had carelessly abandoned over the sofa, tugged my arms through the leather sleeves, and was halfway out the door when a lythe form barrelled past; fingers snatching at my arm to pull me along with him.

"Keane, for Christ's sake—" The hand grew all the more firm as we neared my companion's newly repaired automobile. Doors flew open. Keys were shoved into the ignition. A motor roared.

And we were off.

It was on that December day I learned the true extent of Keane's driving capabilities. The brief patches of snow or ice across the road posed no hazard as we flew along. Twice I was convinced the local police force would find our remains severed and charred at the foot of a frozen cliff; however, a quick flick of the steering wheel soon righted ourselves once more.

Though my confusion appeared infinitely further from the path of reality.

I saw the shops first; the signs forewarning what was left to come. Keane's foot lightened slightly upon the pedal when life began to seep gradually around us in the form of rattled, old automobiles. The great arteries of interlocking streets, perfectly clear for some time, suddenly thickened and clogged with a mass of people bending over the other to gawk at the throbbing centre.

A heart-attack.

Keane leapt from behind the steering wheel and pushed his way through the crowd, where a few more daring bystanders curled around the sight that would haunt me for several fortnights to come.

Reggie Severtson lay on his back; eyes wide and sightless as his entire body jerked uncontrollably against the pavement. Limbs flailed dangerously in every direction. A thin, bubbling stream of saliva spewed over the youth's cracked lips.

Keane dropped his canvas rucksack beside the child and turned to the grocer.

"When did the seizure start?"

"A few minutes after I rang you." The aproned man stated. "Thought he was just being a normal ruffian—raving about monsters and birds coming out of the walls—but then he just collapsed." My companion took out a small torch from his pocket and pointed it into the boy's sightless eyes.

"And you called an ambulance?"

"Right when the shaking started."

"Good. Lawrence, help me get him on his side." Together, Keane and I gingerly rolled the youth on one shoulder. The wild motions in his arms did not cease, though his desperate breaths were at least improved by the action. My companion tore the leather strap of his watch from around his wrist. The timepiece was pressed into my hands.

"Start counting."

And so I did; seconds kept silently in my head as Keane observed the uncontrollable writhing against the pavement. My companion's lack of overcoat required him to remove his tweed jacket instead; rolling it up beneath the brown-haired head before it bashed against the pavement. The taste of blood warmed my mouth, but I kept counting in synchronization with the thin hand of Keane's wristwatch. A bowl of water had been called for and brought forward. My companion submerged a handkerchief and placed it over Reggie Severtson's brow. This was repeated in almost exact thirty-second intervals until the screams of mechanical sirens appeared and the boy's desperate contortions at last calmed into a limp, groggy state.

"Lawrence, time."

"Three minutes and fifty-four seconds." Keane nodded and helped the uniformed medics gingerly move the child onto the stretcher. Being that Reggie Severtson was neither light, nor lithe, it took slightly more effort than one might have expected; however, he was soon tucked in the back of the wailing chariot. My companion clambered in behind the metal cot. A set of keys flew toward me, caught easily in one palm.

"Meet me at the hospital."

I nodded once, gripped the key ring more firmly between my fingers, and looked up to give some words of assurance.

But they were of no use.

The ambulance was gone.

CHAPTER FOUR

I have never liked hospitals. The odours of bleach and vomit always left me feeling ill, even though it was not I strapped down by tubes and needles.

No, I have never liked hospitals.

My path down the blandly painted walls was lined with faded loops of paper bound together in a chain. Each individual was as a bed stationed in every sterilized room. Should its inhabitant die, the chain of life would break.

But it would not end.

The piece would be replaced. The bed would be refilled.

Life would continue.

As though it never stopped.

I wrapped my arms tightly about myself; fingers gripping into the thick leather. The keys in my jacket pocket were the only abnormality, and yet it still fit somehow. It was as though nothing was out of place.

While everything crumbled and fell.

It took a few attempts of my feet—a few directions muddled in the chaos of my mind—but I eventually found the single room offset slightly from the continuous row of identical spaces.

Of course, it wasn't too difficult to distinguish as soon as I turned the corner.

Not every room had Keane stationed outside; sitting straight and rigid in a chair no doubt supplied by a lower of the hospital staff.

I dropped the ring of keys on top of his strategically folded hands.

My companion, in spite of his stiff posture, roused slowly from his thoughts; tentatively wrapping his fingers around the cut metal and staring up at me as though awakened from a long, hellish sleep.

"You shouldn't have come." I shrugged.

"You told me to meet you here, so I did." My heart stopped. "Christ, he hasn't—"

"No. No, Reggie will be alright. In time." Every breath of air I had inhaled from the moment Keane dragged me out of the cottage to this sorry excuse of a conversation rushed from my lungs in one, enormous heave; leaving me little to do but lean against the wall. My silence was not entirely futile, however. When Keane reached into his pockets, only to discover his silver cigarette case remained in the jacket he had lent to young Severtson's head, I was able to pass down a fresh package I carried for just such occasions.

"Have his parents been informed?"

A thin cigarette balanced between his fingers.

"I made certain of it."

"But they aren't here."

Keane swept his lighter beneath the end of the rolled tobacco, inhaled deeply, and allowed the first, thin trail of smoke to billow upwards above his head.

"No."

With that single word—just one syllable—something rusted and old snapped within the fabric of my being.

"You would think the mother would be gloating over her son's illness."

"Lawrence—"

"I mean, really, Keane. She wanted you to diagnose him, and now you can." I had not realised just how rapidly my arms were moving through the air until a hand reached up and lightly rested on my forearm. My companion rose from the chair, causing me to once again take position as the shorter. The less wise. The foolish.

I felt like a child.

"Amphetamine."

"Pardon?"

"Amphetamine." Keane repeated. "I assume you have heard of it?"

"Isn't it a drug?"

"More than that, Lawrence. Much more. Amphetamine can be used for various purposes: neurotic depression; improve wakefulness; increase energy—"

"A miracle drug then?" My companion's head tipped to one side; searching my face for a moment before allowing his brow to brush against the wall.

"There is no such thing as a 'miracle drug'. Even penicillin has its faults. For every cure found, there are a thousand evils."

"But some evils are necessary."

"Are they?" The back of my throat suddenly became cracked and dry around my tongue. Of course, some evils were necessary. We were fighting an entire war over the subject. It was a shame to lose good men, but should one good man kill a thousand bad men before his death, it would have been a victory. Yes, people were dying. Yes, it was a horrid event forever to mar the books yet to come.

But it was necessary.

Wasn't it?

Keane cleared his throat.

"The trouble with children is that they are often susceptible to the ideals of others. They think of their forefathers' mistakes as victories, and their blood as smiles. That boy in there had to get those tablets from somewhere. More than that, he must have had a reason for swallowing them. There is very little difference, Lawrence, between knowledge and stupidity. He must have seen someone take the tablets, seen the improved psychological effects, and decided to do the same. It was his choice. It was a poor one, but it was his. However, if you look close enough, you might just see a sad little boy who wants to be happy."

"But where would a child that age learn about amphetamine?" The words were still carefully formulating in Keane's head when his eyebrows shot up and he nodded behind me.

"I believe your answer has just arrived."

The heavy huffing of overworked lungs echoed down the hallway. Again, it was Keane to draw the tear-soaked woman to the correct room.

"Where's my Reggie?"

"Ah, Mrs. Severtson. Your son is resting comfortably right now. If you would care to sit down—"

"I don't want to sit. I want to see my Reggie." The stout woman pushed past the chair, though she did not make it around my companion's outstretched arm.

"You must wait a moment. The doctor is with him now."

"Doctor?" She whispered breathlessly. It was as though a trained physician was somehow a rarity in hospitals. All at once her knees began to tremble, and she would have fallen dramatically on Keane, had he not bore the foresight to lead her to the chair pushed still against the wall. For a woman who raved about visiting medical experts in London, she was certainly moved by a general practitioner working out of a small hospital.

"There." Keane handed the weeping woman his handkerchief. She stared at the white cloth, then at my companion. "Might as well wipe your eyes. You wouldn't want your son to see you crying, would you? Or your husband?" Another heavy sob erupted through the woman; however, rather than simply stifling the onslaught of tears in the handkerchief between her meaty fingers, she reached desperately for Keane's sleeve.

"You won't tell Sebastion of this, will you?" This was not said as a question, but a desperate cry for help from a shipwreck victim who learned the moment they hit the water they did not know how to swim. My companion squatted down by the arm of the chair.

"Mrs. Severtson, what sort of gentleman would I be if I informed your husband of a few tears? It is against my rule as an Irishman." I caught the slight twist of Keane's mouth as he briefly mentioned the land of his birth. The woman in the chair; however, saw nothing but a life preserved being tossed into the ocean.

"Oh, thank you, Professor!"

"Not at all." My companion assured her as he cautiously leaned on his heels to escape the possible fate of two arms flinging around his shoulders and holding him against her chest. "If I may venture one question though?"

"Anything."

"Does Mr. Severtson hurt you?"

"I'll have you know Sebastian has not once raised a hand to me or my son. The very thought—" Keane raised his hand.

"I understand he may not physically harm you, but emotionally perhaps. Tell me, has he ever said anything cruel toward you? Not the standard marital quarrels, but something truly hurtful to either you or young Reggie?"

An enormous wail broke once more through the general quiet of the hospital; subsiding, not completely, but just enough to decipher the grim distinctness of words from hysterical babbling.

"He has. Often too." She paused to wipe her nose. "He . . . he says I'm fat. I know I could stand to lose a few stone, Sir. I know I am not as slim as I was the day we were married, but does that give him any right to gallivant about with another woman?" Keane tugged at his ear.

"Are you quite certain he is, as you say, with another woman? Your husband does keep long working hours." The woman shook her head.

"A wife knows. I've seen the lipstick on his collar. He reeks of cheap perfume when he comes to bed. If he comes home at all." I had thought this to be the end, but Mrs. Severtson continued without prompting. "I tried to lose a bit of weight, but I didn't know the way about it. I've never been very good at athletics. Then a friend of mine, she told me about these tablets that helped her after she had her boy. My stomach, though, has never been too strong with medicines, and the little things just kept me awake at night or feeling ill most of the time."

"So, you stopped using them. How long ago was that?"

"A month or two. A week before my Reggie began having his little fits. Oh, my lord! Reggie!" The woman's attempt to rise from the small hospital chair were thwarted by Keane's arm.

"He will be alright, Mrs. Severtson. The dosage wasn't high enough to do any lasting damage."

"Thank God." She gasped, clutching at a string of pearls running about her neck. "I didn't think those little tablets were dangerous."

"In large amounts, any drug is dangerous. Your son seems to have been ingesting small doses for some time, which built up to the incident we are now witnessing."

"You mean, those pills are what has been causing his extra energy?"

"Precisely."

"So he isn't mental?"

"No." Whatever relief was exhaled from the woman as the weight of weeks' worth of concern fell away was immediately replaced by a distinct redness to her face.

"My husband said some horrible things to Reggie a few weeks ago. About the time all this started. Do you think that could have caused this?"

"Perhaps." Keane's eyebrows furrowed together until they were one. "Does he often insult your son?"

"Constantly. Sebastion's idea of a man is what he can take from life, without consequence or consideration."

"And you *married* this man?" I couldn't stop them. The words simply slipped from my mouth and landed on the floor with a heavy thud. The woman turned to me; brow lowered slightly. This, I thought, was more likely an action of concentration, rather than anger toward my bluntness.

"Miss Lawrence, is it?" I nodded. "Miss Lawrence, I was never like you when I was a young woman. I thought more about what men thought about me than I thought about myself, let alone my brains. I met a man, and he seemed to like me well enough, so we married. My only excuse is my feet were knocked out from under me by his charm. Don't make my mistake. When you find a man and he proposes, you make sure you have both feet firmly under you before you say 'yes.'" I would have said something, if indeed I could have found the words to say anything, had the doctor not returned and allowed Mrs. Severtson to move to her son's side.

I followed Keane red faced out to his awaiting motorcar, clambered into the seat, and allowed the metal machine to pull away from the place of bleach and tears.

MRS. MCCARTHY SWEPT our coats away the moment we stepped through the cottage door. Keane had offered to drive me to my own flat; however, I found the welcome of his housekeeper's fine cooking to be far more profitable than the accursed crumble of an empty pantry. A hot stew was placed before us; thickly laden with vegetables, rather than the meat so desired by such recipes. For the bits of beef that had managed to sneak into the pot, we were most thankful.

Keane and I also received many threats of what kitchen utensils we would find flying at our heads, should we ever dare to miss lunch again.

My companion's half-hearted promise was far more convincing than my own mutterings around a mouth full of the lovely stew.

Cups of tea were poured and carried to the study, along with a few holiday goods baked in our absence. I immediately rediscovered my place on the sofa, while Keane took a somewhat longer route to his own armchair.

"Are you thoughtful, Lawrence, or merely tired?"

"Both actually." I replied, sitting a little straighter. "It has been a long day."

"Indeed, it has. But also, I think, a profitable one. I dare say Mrs. Severtson will not bow to her husband so easily now."

"No. No, probably not. Won't that cause some problems, though?"

"In what way?"

"Well, it's a little like a revolution, isn't it?" I asked. "It isn't as though either side will willingly concede to another without a fight. All we might have done is start two people on the path of divorce." Keane seemed to take this thought seriously for a moment before chuckling.

"Lawrence, you believe every marriage ends in divorce."

"Not everyone." I defended. "But many do, or would if people found it more acceptable. Besides, you have no right to talk. You're a bachelor." My companion paused midway between lighting a cigarette to stare at me. Eventually the need of the match won out, and a soft wave of tobacco soon marked the end of the motion.

But certainly not the end of a thought.

"You claimed we may have had a hand at a revolution, but isn't that all life is? Sometimes it takes a bit of bloodshed to prove what we should have known from the beginning."

"And that is?" Keane sighed and brought the cigarette away from his lips.

"We should—What is it Mrs. McCarthy?" I had not heard the housekeeper's entrance, but, when I did, I could not understand how I had missed it. Mrs. McCarthy is not a woman to be shaken; however, I did not believe it was the waning light that made her so pale, nor the late hour a reason to twist one's hands together so tightly.

"There's a gentleman coming up the drive, Sir. Sure, but he's a bad one, so he is. Stumbling about half gone. Would you be wanting to see him?" Keane crushed the glowing end of a scarcely touched cigarette into a nearby ashtray.

"No, but let him in anyway."

"But Keane, if it's Severtson—"

"Then you will say nothing, Lawrence. Heaven knows hot tempers have never solved anything, and I find myself a bit too tired for a drunken brawl in my own house, let alone having to peel you off of some corpse. No, there will be no grave digging tonight." I at least recognised the last phrase to be a jest, yet, in my knowledge of this, I also caught the iron glint hiding at the back of Keane's eyes.

All too soon, Sebastian Severtson staggered through the doors.

He was not how I pictured him, if I indeed imagined him at all. He was not some enormous brute of a man, but instead scrawny with a balding head of brown hair greased to cover the more bare of spots. A full business suit was crumpled against his frame as he swayed just a few feet from my companion. Keane's lips tightened into something a great deal more threatening than a smile.

"Ah, Mr. Severtson. I do hope this is a brief visit."

"You talked to my wife."

"I converse with your wife on several occasions. Which might this be?" An unsteady finger jutted out toward Keane's face.

"Today. At the hospital. You told her to leave me."

"I did no such thing."

"You did, and now she says she wants to take the boy and run off for two months. At least."

"Every woman needs a holiday."

"To their mum's. No, Professor. I'm no idiot. I could lose money over this."

"Is that all you think about: money?" The man turned around unsteadily toward me. His eyes were concealed by the thick fog of intoxication.

"Who the hell are you?" Gradually the blurriness of his pupils dissipated somewhat; allowing the fog to surround his brain instead. "Oh, you're the Professor's girl, eh? I always said he couldn't be a bachelor completely." Keane reacted before my fist was given a chance.

"I must ask you to leave, Sir. Now." Instead, Severtson did the complete opposite. He staggered further toward me and reaching an arm out—

CRACK!

Amazing what little pain one feels in their hand when adrenaline rushes in. As I opened my eyes, I found the intruder to be sprawled backward on the floor with a fresh streak of blood pooling from his lip. I looked aghast at my own fingers, then even more so at the knuckles Keane was nursing with his unaffected hand.

"Christ." I gasped. My companion glanced at me, then down to the grown man weeping on the carpet.

A slight redness gradually crept along his ears to match the angry tint of his sore hand.

"Lawrence, I am afraid we may need that shovel after all."

CHAPTER FIVE

-Christmas Day, 1941-

"YOU NEVER ANSWERED my question." Keane glanced up from the glass of Irish whiskey he had been nursing between his long fingers for some time; a heavy book of ancient philosophy laid open in his lap.

"And which question would that be? I often fear your curiosity will be the death of me."

"The one I asked the day you knocked Mr. Severtson out on the rugs." How long had it been since then? Days? A week? It didn't seem so. I could still recall every detail vividly. Keane's slight embarrassment as Mrs. McCarthy entered to find a grown man out cold across the floor. The weight of Severtson's legs as we carried him to the motorcar. The stench of alcohol that stubbornly remained in upholstery for days. I even recalled the vivid curses slurred from the man's mouth as Keane and I dumped him at the feet of his rather unexpecting cleaning lady.

Yes, I remembered that day.

How could I forget it?

Keane's lips twitched slightly.

"You mean the question about rebellion?" I nodded.

"Exactly. You said a little bloodshed can prove what we should have always known, yet you never told me what that certain bit of knowledge is. Certainly, you are not thinking we ought to revolt at every little discrepancy of opinions."

"Of course not, but that does bring about a good point."

"Which is?" Keane closed his book to allow him to settle further against the back of his armchair.

"Have you heard from young Reggie lately?"

"Not lately. Are you changing the subject?"

"No. I am merely providing proof."

"Of what? Good lord, Keane, am I going to have to drag every little answer out of you?" My companion had at least the grace to smile at this before reaching into the inner pocket of his suit jacket to extract, not his cigarette case, but a thin envelope bearing his name and address on one side.

It was passed to me.

"This arrived two or three days ago in the post. You'll notice the postal address."

"From Sussex."

"Yes, it seems Mrs. Severtson's mother lives there. Beautiful place, Sussex. Does wonders for the soul." I nodded half-heartedly; fully aware just how ironic it was for a devoted Irishman, who admittedly bore the accent of an Englishman, to praise a countryside other than that of his birth.

My eyes swept over the first piece of paper. A letter.

"She does seem much happier." Keane offered as he sipped at his whiskey.

"Much." I agreed. "And Reggie has taken up sport?"

"Seems the child wants to take up boxing. Admittedly, he is a bit young to start up now, but in a few years' time, he will be a fine specimen in the ring."

"And what is this?" I held up the second piece of paper with a grin. A sketch took up much of the page, though the hand with which it was drawn, while incredibly skilled, was not quite so impressive as the picture itself.

I stifled a laugh behind the palm of my hand.

"Good lord, it's you."

And indeed, it was.

Every sharp feature of my companion's face was expertly laid out against the dimensionless page. The slight bend to his Roman nose. Lines engraved along his forehead. Protruding cheekbones with slightly more hollowed cheeks. Thin lips pressed together and curled upwards slightly at the edges. Every hair styled close against his head was given singular definition, while at the same point blurring into controlled waves along with the others.

Then there were the eyes.

Perfectly matching to the two observing me just a few yards away, the eyes were the exact reflection of life. A bit of lightness near the top of the pupil expressed a constant amusement; as though the after effect of some great jest.

The lines below the eyes were another matter.

Deep and darkly shaded, one could not ignore the shadows of sadness captured in an otherwise pleasant expression.

But it had always been that way, hadn't it?

No matter the joy, no matter the excitement, Keane would always carry his past, just as I carried mine. There were no exceptions to his grief. There were no keys for me to unlock the infinite cabinets of his mind and wander back to a time I would never be able to see with my own eyes. It is strange to be bound so deeply to another human being—to know every breath before the lungs take notice—and yet realise the person you have come to rely upon is little more than a glorified stranger.

I passed both pages back to Keane, who took his time memorizing each detail of the sketch.

"Mrs. Seberton made it." He explained offhandedly. "It is not a bad piece, all and all, though I do not believe the likeness to be exact. She has been far too lax about my age and overly generous to the contours of my face as a whole." I shrugged.

"I think it is rather good. She captured your eyes well." A greying eyebrow lurched upward.

"Did she indeed? Well, that is a blessing, I suppose." Keane reopened the book across his legs, all the while pausing every so often to drink the liquor still left in his glass.

It was only when he rose to pour himself another draught, I realised what he had done.

I groaned.

"Keane, you distracted me again."

"And I am afraid I must do so once more, Lawrence, for it seems I have forgotten to give you your Christmas present." My companion grinned at my frustration as he strode slowly—ever so slowly—to his desk, pulled a paper-wrapped parcel from one of the drawers, and carried it dramatically to me.

There was not, a hasten to say, anything strictly unusual about the outer coverings by which the gift itself was obscured. The paper was brown; tied together with a long piece of white twine with little stripes.

I slipped my finger under the knot on top, only to set the parcel aside once more.

"No. No, I will not open it until you explain to me just what humanity has forgotten."

"Very well." Keane leaned against the mantlepiece; fresh glass of whiskey balancing in one hand. When nothing was said for more than a strict thirty seconds, I thought I had played my cards poorly. Then my companion graciously began. "Compassion, Lawrence. That is what we have forgotten."

"Compassion?" Surely it couldn't be that simple.

"Yes. The other day, though I cannot recall exactly which one, you asked if you should feel compassion toward the Nazis. Now I must answer by saying you *should not* feel compassion toward them. Instead, you *must*. Understand that not every boy we shoot down, or shoots us down, wants to be on the battlefield that day. They were forced by the cruelness of others. Perhaps their family was threatened. Their land. Their home. Perhaps they themselves would have been executed for not taking up arms against us. To them, we are the enemy, while we ourselves feel our cause righteous and just."

"But aren't we?" I asked hopefully. "Not completely, of course, but Hitler—"

"Ah, yes. Herr Hitler. Admittedly he is the cause for much of this mess. Certainly, he has killed millions, and for that I dare say compassion is a great deal harder." My companion downed a large portion of his glass, rolled the rim around between his fingers, and continued a bit more slowly than before. "You are, I think, too young to recall the effects of the last war. No one may hold it against you. It is simply a matter of years and days. Allow me to say then that our actions—the United States' and Britain's'—were less than understanding toward Germany. You have heard of the Treaty of Versailles? Yes? In theory, it was made to pay for the war; to somehow compensate for allowing hundreds of thousands of men to slaughter each other in trenches dug by their own hands. We did not wish to pay. We did not wish to acknowledge the pain of loss. Therefore, we left it up to the Germans; throwing them into an economic depression and us—"

"Into a second war. I . . . I think I understand now."

"Do you? If so, I must congratulate you for comprehending what men in Parliament do not. I must also ask a question."

"And that is?" Keane's eyes drilled into my face.

"How are you going to apply that knowledge?"

"How am I going to—"

"Apply the knowledge, yes. You are an intelligent young woman. Not smart. *Intelligent*. There is a difference. People who are merely smart inhale knowledge well enough, but they never draw the connections between what they read and what they live. You, my dear Lawrence, are intelligent, and I expect you to act as such."

I was, for a rare moment in my life, without words at all.

I could neither speak nor understand the great vastness of the complement put before me, just as I found my mouth unable to form a reciprocal kindness.

Keane glanced at his watch and separated his arm from the mantlepiece.

"It is late. I will go tell Mrs. McCarthy we are ready for supper. You will stay, of course? Good." My companion tapped the unwrapped parcel still in my hands with the pad of his thin forefinger. "You might as well open this in my absence. It does no one good to remain otherwise." I did manage to nod there, gaining a slight smile before Keane disappeared from the study.

With a sudden cautiousness I was unaware it was possible for me to possess, I again slipped my hand beneath the knot of twine and gingerly pulled away the stripes. I paused slightly when the brown paper alone was left between my curiosity and it's solvent, but eventually I pulled that layer away as well.

My hands immediately set to running along the cover and binding; caressing it as though made of golden plates, rather than paper and glue.

Indeed, it was not so much of a surprise to me that it was a book than it was new. New. The binding remained untouched, save by that of my own hands at that very moment. I opened the book at the beginning and immediately allowed the pages to flit past as a blur. And then I did it again—more slowly this time—until my eyes once more caught what I had thought to be an illusion first.

A photograph.

I was not so vain as to expect my own face to stare back at me, but I have always been quick to admire art.

And art it was.

The cliffs of Devon portrayed in scales of grey as the summer waters lapped somewhere below. It was neither sunset, nor sunrise. It was not as poetic as that. The sun was but a spot in the sky.

A pinprick.

And yet, all the life and light on earth derived from that single injury.

I removed the photograph and caught sight of the line hiding just behind.

I SEE BARSAD, AND CLY, Defarge, The Vengeance, the Juryman, the Judge, long ranks of the new oppressors who have risen on the destruction of the old, perishing by this retributive instrument, before it shall cease out of its present use. I see a beautiful city and brilliant

people rising from this abyss, and, in their struggles to be truly free, in their triumphs and defeats, through long long years to come, I see the evil of this time and of the previous time of which this is the natural birth, gradually making explanation for itself and wearing it out.

"LAWRENCE?" I STARTED up from the sofa with book and photograph both clutched in my arms as I faced my companion.

"Thank you."

"It is only a book."

As if there was ever 'only a book'.

Keane smiled kindly and strode over to gently extract the gift from my hands; laying both gently down on the seat I had so quickly vacated.

"Now, Mrs. McCarthy has supper laid on the table, and I fear her patience has not improved, in spite of the holiday season." I followed my companion out of the study, but not before glancing back once more through the open doors to the brown paper and twine lying on the floor and the book sitting in the midst of a thousand of its kin lined on shelves along the walls.

IT IS A FAR, FAR BETTER thing that I do, than I have ever done; it is a far, far better rest that I go to, than I have ever known.

AND SUCH WAS "A TALE of Two Cities".

Such was the understanding of two acquaintances.

AUTHOR'S NOTICE

There is something to be said of novellas. One is not forced to carefully plan devastating plots, nor maul over pages of scenes of structured scripts or sharp movements.

One is merely asked to sit.

Sip a cup of tea.

And relax.

And what better time is there to do so than the great holiday season?

Really, this story is not so much based on the problems of the Severtson family (though clearly there are many), but instead it allows a peek into the early years of Lawrence and Keane's acquaintanceship. Moments of domesticity, seldom shown, are gradually brought to light through simple preparations for Christmas. It is a side I had not planned.

Even so, I do not believe myself entirely disappointed in the outcome.

I must also state that the lack of compassion—of kindness—in this world is not a problem contained to that of the past, but remains very real in our lives today.

There are still people out there who endeavour to be kind, but they are much more rare than before; sparkling diamonds created from coal as they were crushed over years of their life. It is often recognised that many of those most desperate to show kindness to others are those who know what a loss the world would have without it. Now we are fighting for each living breath; arguing over morality and ethics I am no longer certain exist. We have developed a superiority complex in our society which dictates that, in order to be worth something, we must make others feel they are nothing. The worst part is that we think we are right.

But are we?

I leave the answer to you, dear reader, as well as wishing you a very Merry Christmas and Happy Holidays.

Did you love *A Very Merry Monster*? Then you should read *The Crimson Shaw*[1] by Elyse Lortz!

[2]

The last thing Joanna Lawrence wishes to do is spend her summer in the United States, even if it is California. Where the lights and glamour may tempt some, she and Professor Brendan Keane find themselves once more facing the side of society kept secure in the shadows. Danger surrounds them constantly, and Keane's old friend, James Harrison, seems to remain in the center of it all. The only question is, what does a high-strung theatre director have to hide? And why is his production of *Pygmalion* turning into a blood-chilling fight between life and death?

1. https://books2read.com/u/mejRRA

2. https://books2read.com/u/mejRRA

Also by Elyse Lortz

Lawrence and Keane
Come Away
The Crimson Shaw
A Very Merry Monster

Poetry for the Wandering Mind
This Midnight Hour

www.ingramcontent.com/pod-product-compliance
Ingram Content Group UK Ltd.
Pitfield, Milton Keynes, MK11 3LW, UK
UKHW040020200726
13854UKWH00001B/290

9 798201 181833